a Fistful of LIFE

a Fistful of LIFE

Krishna Datta

Srishti
PUBLISHERS & DISTRIBUTORS

SRISHTI PUBLISHERS & DISTRIBUTORS
64-A, Adhchini
Sri Aurobindo Marg
New Delhi - 110 017

Published in 1999 by
SRISHTI PUBLISHERS & DISTRIBUTORS

Rs. 95.00
ISBN : 81-87075-41-4

Typeset in 13.5 on 16.5pt Palatino by S Kumar at Srishti

Printed and bound in India by
Saurabh Print-O-Pack, NOIDA (U.P.).

Contents

Chapter 1 1

Chapter 2 23

Chapter 3 47

Chapter 4 55

Chapter 5 75

Chapter 6 85

Chapter 7 93

ONE

CHAPTER

It is no mean feat that Suchitra, Suchi for short, aged sixteen, has managed to leave two marriages behind her. It appears to the household, where she works as a cook-cum-maid servant, that she does not give a damn about it either. It is a source of great amusement to the employer's family – they often have a hearty laugh at her expense. Suchi giggles with them, covering her mouth with her sari. They tell guests, 'Do you know ...' In time their hilarity would turn into persistent disbelief 'Well, we would have never thought ...'

The village they live in is no longer a sleepy and quiet place. There is only one pucca road in the village where all the buses run, the lorries blow air-horns that pierce the villager's eardrums, the van-rickshaws and the three-wheelers belch diesel fumes to their heart's content, plying to and fro from the Dimna railway station. Adding to the fume and noise are the cycle-rickshaws fitted with loudspeakers that continuously announce the introduction of a new soap or hair oil in the market or the latest film that is being shown in the only cinema hall at Dimna. In winter, the loudspeakers insist the villagers come out and see the thrilling yatra that has been imported from – where else but – Calcutta! It goes on blaring: *Sashane Lakkhi Kandche* – the Goddess Laxmi is weeping in the crematorium. At times, there is no reprieve, even at night. The non-stop Hari Sankirtan *Hare hare Krishna krishna, krishna krishna Hare Hare* – is chanted over loudspeakers for three days and three nights running.

The womenfolk of the house take Suchi along to see plays from Calcutta. They sit on chairs, Suchi on a torn mat laid out on the ground. Suchi loves a good show. She becomes so engrossed that in the very last act, when the real culprit is identified in public, she throws her chappal at the hapless actor. Soon the rest of the audience joins the fray of chappal – throwing with a great enthusiasm. The victim leaves the stage in a huff and runs to save his dear life. 'Serves him right!' Suchi screams. The curtain falls quickly. After the show, the organisers come on the stage and express their displeasure at the reaction of the audience. Then the scramble starts for retrieving the chappals, cheap plastic vanity-bags, umbrellas or whatever. Suchi cuts her losses and goes home with her employers, only one of her chappals in her hand. It's worth it, she concludes.

Suchi loves her village Dimna. The noise and bustle does not bother her at all. She has seen the woods disappear and the sleepy village come to life with people. The Bangladeshees with their green fingers had covered the field with cauliflowers, cabbages, green chillies, hard mounted their thatched roofs with pumpkin creepers. Sitting on the matted ground she had seen a few travelling filmshows too. Now there is a new pucca cinema hall in the village as well as the video parlour in a tent, where a few rickety chairs and mats are placed on the barren ground. But most of all, she loves the river Didar that flows parallel to the busy mainroad with a sluggish unconcern. The current is deep in the middle and the boatmen row their country boats with no apparent hurry. The two river banks speak almost of two different cultures: the solid brick houses dotted with trees on one side and the sleepy village with mud houses and abundant vegetation challenging the ruthless development of Didar, on the other.

In her childhood, which seems ages ago, she had been a wild, carefree little girl who had always managed to look unwashed even after a swim in the river. Her mother had indeed tried to make Suchi literate. She had sent her to the local pathshala consisting of a makeshift room, where young children of all ages from the poorer families sat on the floor. They rocked on their tiny, skinny bottoms and recited after the pandit –' two and two four, four and four eight ...' Suchi was not unwillng to learn the tables, it was easy enough for her. She had picked up the Bengali alphabet in no time. But she found it very boring to go on repeating after the pandit once she had learnt it all by heart. What really tried her limited patience, however, was having to massage the pandit's dirty feet almost everyday. Why, among all the children, was she chosen to do this service was a mystery to her.

One day, on her way to the pathshala, she picked up a few Chotra leaves. That day, to the pandit's surprise, she volunteered to massage his feet. She massaged the legs with the mustard oil first, then rubbed the leaves on the soles of his feet. The poor man was dozing off when he leapt up with a scream and fell flat on his face. Before he could sit up and look for his cane, Suchi had melted into thin air, never to be seen anywhere near the place. The pandit could not teach for a week: his feet were swollen like footballs and God did it itch! He had to be carried away by a van-rickshaw. He cursed Suchi, her fourteen generations of forefathers and the fourteen to come, all the way home.

For once, Suchi thought she had deserved the thrashing from her mother. Next morning, with her bruised body, she had to go to the nearby pond to scrub the pots and pans and aluminium plates. The women and the girls who came to the pond to wash their clothes, scrub their utensils and to take an early morning dip – all looked at Suchi and laughed. Scrap of a thing! Where did she get the nerve to play such a trick: to rub chotra leaves on the pandit's feet. Suchi giggled back, unashamed.

Her next chore was to fetch drinking water from the tube-well, half-a-kilometere away. She just about managed to carry the earthen container on her hip, splashing water all the way back to the hut.

Her mother told her to sweep and mop the floor with cow-dung liquid, feed her ailing father, wash the clothes, cut the vegetables before she left for work. Mother usually took Tuki, the five-year-old daughter, with her, but that day she left her with Suchi, 'Look after Tuki' she called out. Suchi was, in other words, truly grounded.

She sang, she danced, she chased a cow which ventured into their courtyard. Feeding father was no problem at all. She dipped the chapaties made the day before in sugared water and gave them to him. The little sister, Tuki, sat on the floor, chewing the chapatis and turning to feed her rag doll alternatively.

When Mother came back, they ate together. The two boy were to come home later. The older boy, a seventeen-year-old, went to the field to work for a farmer. The younger, a eleven-year-old went to a regular school. For a few days, Suchi stayed at home and worked. Her mother thought that the tide had really turned. Thank God, no more complaints pouring in every day of the week!

One Saturday afternoon when mother came

home from work she found her daughter missing. All the house work had been done, Tuki was fast asleep on her father's bed, but Suchi was nowhere to be seen.

Saturdays were big days in Dimna. Goods arrived from the surrounding villages – the farmers with their rice lentils, vegetables, seasonal fruits, fresh sweet-water fish, goatmeat, and ready made clothes, saris – retailers and wholesalers all thronged together. Tea and snack-stalls mushroomed everywhere and bhaji-wallahs set up their shops in the market place. Suchi gave free service to one of the tea-stall holders. She loved serving tea to the weary shoppers and listening to their excited talk. And before dusk settled and the market packed up, she had savoured her well-deserved glass of tea and gone home. She seldom got tipped and when she did, gave it to the stall-holder. Suchi always went home happy, humming the latest tune picked up from the market place. She never filched any thing from the market: that was not her style.

She stole from the trees. Her father had told her that God had created this world. What about the trees she had asked. 'Everything, everybody,' he had told her. No seasonal fruits were safe from Suchi's tiny hands. She would climb trees like the neighbourhood monkeys. In winter, at the crack of dawn, she would go out in search of date juice, her favourite drink. She would climb a tree, drink from the pot to her heart's content and leave it the way it was. The owner might spot her from afar, but she would slide down and vanish before he could catch her.

What she loved most was the river Didar. Her favourite sport was to jump into the river from the raised bank, listen to the sound of the splash she made, feel the water gurgling all around her, over her. She would startle the anglers, breaking their rods, freeing the fish and swimming underwater to the opposite bank, laughing her little head off. At times the enraged anglers would threaten her with the broken rod, gleeful at the thought of breaking it on her back and how!

A stick would break on her back alright when she would come home in the afternoons. The mother would shake her head in despair. She could understand a boy getting up to all kinds of mischief but a girl – never. She would starve Suchi, beat her black and blue – but nothing seemed to work. Suchi was just as incorrigible as ever. Mother would tell her and other people that she should have smothered Suchi with a pillow when she was born, like some mothers in the village did when a girl was born to them.

The maths teacher of the local school was feared and respected by everyone. Suchi's mother heard through the grapevine that his wife was looking for a helping hand. She went and talked to the wife. The pay was fixed for rupees fifteen a month and it was agreed that mother would come and collect it at the end of each month. She assured the teacher's wife that Suchi was a good worker even if she was inclined to be wayward. They were free to discipline her as they pleased, she added.

She took Suchi one afternoon to the teacher's modest two-storey house. Suchi accompanied her without a murmur. She was not work-shy. She had to work at home, and now, she would work at somebody else's house. What's the big deal, she reckoned?

So she went with her mother and stood in the walled courtyard, open to the sky. She looked around. She saw the cow-shed, the two trees reaching for the sky with green coconuts clustered around the top – and she wondered if they would be too tall for her to climb. She noticed the tube-well on the raised cemented floor, the dirty pots and pans and dishes lying around a young boy brushing his teeth inside the house. The boy caught her dancing eyes as she cried out: 'O ma, look! he looks like an owl' and at once she felt a stinging slap in her face and heard the hiss: 'Shut up'. She did shut up but not before she could stifle a giggle with her tiny hand.

The teacher's wife looked at her – a skinny, scruffy little girl, hair all over her face, wearing a printed frock two sizes too big for her, flapping like a tent in the wind. She smiled at Suchi. Doubtful, Suchi smiled back. She was hired. Suchi hummed and sang, ran up and down the stairs and did much more than she was asked to. As soon as the teacher came home cycling, she ran to greet him with a glass of water. There was no question of taming Suchi, everyone was delighted to have such a willing worker. Surely there was no wickedness in her? She scrubbed and washed the dirty utensils, filled the buckets with water, jumping up and down with the handle to collect it from the tube-well. She swept and mopped the entire house, and was forever fetching things in a house full of people. 'Suchi get me a glass of water'... 'Suchi, where have my shoes gone? ... Bring me this and bring me that – the smiling face of Suchi would appear and disappear like a flash of lightning.

The honeymoon lasted almost two weeks. She came to work at seven in the morning and left promptly at four-thirty in the afternoon. No amount of persuasion could keep her after that. This was a record achievement for Suchi; only her mother knew that. Suddenly, one Saturday, late morning, she went missing. 'Suchi! Suchi!' her name reverberated throughout the house. This started happening once, twice, thrice a week. She would go missing for a couple of hours; on Saturdays, for the whole day. She would come back as if nothing had happened and look genuinely surprised when she was ticked off. She would pout as if she was going to cry and then burst into giggles. She got regular warnings from the teacher's wife: 'If you do that again, you need not come back, do you understand? ' and she would nod her head, looking at the cows. However, missing she went but come back she did, too. The usual complaint, the expected beating from the mother, nothing could stop her from going off again. Her mother would say that Suchi had the bones of a cat – they never broke.

Once, the fishermen found her when their boat was in mid-river appearing like a ghost from under the planks. It was too late to go back and dump her, so she sailed with them. Her feet and dress wet and dirtied. But she sat quietly as if she belonged to the boat while the fishermen spread the huge net in the river with deft hands. The sun was pouring down. Suchi watched the shining silver water, looked at the reflections of the trees, and the moving cloud. She looked up at the blue sky and she saw a line of birds flying away. She smiled. She wished she was a bird – free and happy as they were.

That evening, she had come home straight from the fishing expedition. It was much too late for her to go back to work anyway. She found the house full with her sisters, nephews and nieces – the children running around all over the place. She was surprised but pleased. She thought she would be able to get away with her afternoon's adventure on the river so she promptly started playing hide and seek with the children. The sleepy dark neighbourhood came alive with laughter and screams. A couple of kerosene lanterns inside the house deepened the shadows. The three older sisters came out smiling. Chiding Suchi affectionately, they called: 'Suchi, stop messing about. Come over.' Except her father, no one ever called out for her sweetly. There was always a note of exasperation in her family's collective voice. She sensed that there must be something terribly wrong. Surely such endearment was uncalled for. She stood there, apprehensive, ready to run for her life. To her eternal regret, she did not escape into the dark night.

Suchi's family had become impoverished by having to fork out dowry for the three daughters. Each time the daughters got married, the father had to sell off bits of his land. Each time the parents cursed their fate for producing five daughters and only two sons.

The eldest, Khuku, was married to a book-keeper. They lived in a semi-pucca house. If anyone asked Khuku or her husband as to what the latter did for a living, they would say with pride that he 'wrote books.' They were happy that in Dimna shops were springing up along the main road. It meant more 'books' for Khuku's husband to 'write', albeit they were for keeping accounts.

The second one, Gita's husband was a stoker in the local brick-field. They lived in a mud house with a little land around it, and just managed to stave off hunger. The husband was always on the look out to make a little extra money.

The third one, Lata, was the luckiest. She was married to a businessman. The youngest son-in-law dealt in 'bekak'. Pray, what kind of black market he indulged in, one might ask? He smuggled cows to Bangladesh across the border, which was only six kilometers away from Dimna. He knew the police and the officers on both sides of the border. He had a monthly arrangement to pay 'toll' and the rest was easy. To acquire this prized son-in-law, Suchi's parents had to pay him rupees five thousand in cash, a cycle, a wrist watch, and a gold ring. For the bride, they had to give four silk sarees, two gold bangles, one gold chain, and a pair of ear-rings. Soon after the wedding, the father took to bed having sold off the last bit of land and his two surviving cows. He never left the bed after that day.

Suddenly, Suchi's future seemed settled for all time to come when an offer came for her hand. Her mother looked on it as god-sent. She had worried a great deal about Suchi's future. Who would ever marry this wayward girl? Even if someone did, where would the money for the dowry come from? They had nothing, absolutely nothing, to sell except the roof over their heads. The stoker son-in-law came one afternoon to talk to Suchi's mother. He would have made a good salesman; he had missed his calling by becoming a stoker. He said that the prospective bride-groom was a cycle-rickshawalla who lived with his mother and brother. What about the father? 'Oh, him?' the stoker son-in-law said airily, 'He went off with another woman. They have got a house near-by, in Shonpur town.' The rickshawalla was willing to pay the bride three hundred rupees. In actual fact, it was four hundred. The stoker had kept aside one hundred as his brokerage fee without revealing it to his mother-in-law. 'Where is the catch? Let alone forgoing dowry, they are actually offering bride-price?' the mother was suspicious. But the stoker reassured her, 'They are town people, progressive, not like us', he said.

The mother called the elder daughters and discussed the pros and cons of the offer with them. They agreed that Suchi was either retarded or simply crazy. No one had ever heard of a girl so wild and so unpredictable – going off with the fishermen, swimming in the river without a stitch, serving tea without taking a paisa from the stallholder. She may get kidnapped any day by a child-lifter and sold off as a prostitute on the streets of Calcutta or made to beg or worse get raped like the eight-year-old Latika and just left in the rice fields to die. They decided that Suchi would be safer married. Besides, they comforted themselves with the stoker's fiction that he knew the family well. So nothing could go wrong if the marriage were to take place. The sisters, especially the cow smuggler's wife, were willing to give her two new silk saris, a couple of cholis and a petticoat. The bride-groom's family did not make any demand whatsoever. Was it not good of them? they said.

Suchi was married off two days later without any fuss. The teacher and his wife vigorously objected to it, pointing out that Suchi was too young, and that it was illegal and detrimental to her health. Whereupon Suchi's mother took hold of Suchi's hand and left their house. Suchi was *her* child, what had the law got to do with all this? Surely, she could do what she liked with her children? As for her growth, the mother, herself, was married at the age of ten. She was alright, wasn't she? Educated people talk nonsense at times, she concluded.

TWO CHAPTER

Suchi had a vague memory of her wedding. She remembered the glass bangles and the tinkling sound they made whenever she moved her hands. However, she recalled hating her mother-in-law's semi-pucca house with a tin roof and one small room and a verendah squashed in the slum.

The little pond nearby was so filthy that she did not even want to wash her feet there. There were hardly any trees and the river was far away. In any case she was not allowed to go out of the house except to fetch drinking water from the neighbouring tube-well.

Suchi had to wait in the queue for an hour, sometimes longer, for water. From time to time a fight would break out when someone tried to jump the queue. How she loved the fights! She too fought not caring whose side she was on – right or wrongs flailing her hands and feet, talking gibberish at the top of her voice. In the middle of a screaming contest it all sounded the same, any way. At that the warring parties would fall silent and gape at her trying to figure out what the hell Suchi was going on about. At this point Such would beam her teeth and make a hasty retreat. The neighbourhood got to know Suchi in no time. She too felt better after fighting other people's battles and went back with the earthen pot, humming a Hindi song. It is good, clean fun, she said to herself.

It was no fun, however, having to spend the nights at her in-laws. A week or so after, the marriage, the mother-in-law told her to sleep in a bed which was in another corner of the room. It was midnight, she was almost dropping off to sleep on her feet. The curtained off corner was her bed-room, she was told. A dim lamp, the only naked light, was still on. She found her crippled brother-in-law Bilku on the wooden bed, grinning from ear to ear, welcoming her with his stumped arms. She asked, wide eyed, 'Where is my bride-groom? He said chuckling: 'From to -day I'm your bride-groom.' 'No, you are not' she screamed and fled before anyone could grab hold of her.

Suchi knew only that a wife should sleep

with her husband and no one else. She was not prepared to compromise on that score. So she ran out of the house, away from the slum and on to the main road. She found a corner-shop, tucked away in the street and climbed on to it's open top. She took off her sari and used it as a pillow and when she felt hot she took off her choli and slept like a log in her petticoat.

Before the town woke up from its slumber the shopkeeper had found her, with vermillon on the parting of her hair, red bangles on her hands – the unmistakeable signs of a newly wed – fast asleep.

'Who are you?' The shopkeeper asked shaking her sleepy, half naked body.

'I am Suchi,' she answered half-asleep.

'Who is your father?' Suchi was quiet.

'Who is your husband? What is his name?'

'I don't know.' Suchi said, bored. In fact she did not know her husband's name. He always woke up late in the morning and once he went out with his rickshaw, he never came home before midnight, sometimes much later. At nightfall, the town became a smugglers' paradise. This was the time to make a few extra rupees for anyone on wheels. Long live the Bangladesh border, said the smugglers, their helpers and the border-security forces.

The shopkeeper threatened to take her to the police station. To the local people the word 'police' was bad news. 'Shun them like poisonous snakes,' she had heard her father say to her elder brother. Suchi tried to run away from the shopkeeper but he caught hold of her wrist. In the tug of war that ensued one red conch-shell bangle broke. The man bit his tongue as it was a bad omen to break the red bangle, but he did not loosen his grip on her.

'Take me to your in-law's house', he commanded.

That was how Suchi came back to her hated in-law's home. As soon as the man left she got the thrashing of her life. She screamed and shouted obscenities to no avail. She understood that mother and mother-in-law were interchangeable as far as thrashings were concerned. The mother-in-law told her that no matter what happened inside the house, she must never ever step out and blacken their name. She was a married woman now and it was up to her to uphold the good reputation of the family. Suchi in turn told her in plain Bengali that if she was made to sleep with the crippled brother-in-law, she would make sure that all the neighbours knew about it, thrashing or no thrashing, regardless of good name.

From then on she became an unpaid servant in the household. The brother-in-law left her alone, but made obscene gestures whenever he saw her. Not to be outdone, Suchi would stick her tongue out at him and giggle. Left to herself, she slept in another corner of the tiny room. She did not mind the house-work, but she did mind not seeing the river, the green fields, the trees, the fruits she used to pluck and eat, the market place, the tea-stall, the customers and her own family. Why did her mother get rid of her? Was she really that bad? She missed her father and her little sister especially. She had always fed them with the fruits she had managed to steal. She of course hotly denied she ever stole. She defiantly declared: 'God has given us trees, hasn't He?'

One night, the mother-in-law told Suchi to go and sleep in the verandah with her husband. The verandah had a tin roof, its sides were open, partly covered by several jute sacks roughly sown together. In one corner there was the kitchen and in the other her husband, Madan, slept on a narrow wooden bed.

During the first few nights, Suchi fought

with Madan for space. He would throw her off the bed and she would crawl under it and go to sleep. One night she woke up feeling chilly so she climbed onto the bed and slept at Madan's feet.

It was early morning. Madan's foot struck her head and she was awake. She then changed her place and slept alongside, putting her arms around him. In her dream she thought of her father and slept the sleep of the innocent.

Suddenly, she felt hot fingers between her legs. She leapt up, wide eyed, and looked at the stranger, bemused. Madan put his fingers on his lips and hissed. He took off his loongi and asked Suchi to suck him. Suck what? What? He forced her little head between his legs and she was amazed to see that this man was no man at all like her brothers. He did not have anything hanging between his legs and he didn't look like a girl either. She covered her face with both her hands and started giggling.

'O ma! what is this?' Suchi cried out. Madan slapped her face and she jumped off the bed and came running to her mother-in-law, who was cooking in the other corner of the same verandah. Suchi sat near her, her head between her knees, and shivered, visibly. She had wanted to reach out to the older woman, to seek her sympathy. But the latter just went on cooking the rice and cutting the vegetables, stonefaced. Suddenly Suchi missed her mother.

In the end Madan won the battle. He used to take ganja, now he started taking country liqour, and felt strong enough to cow down the skinny little body. He tied her hands and feet with rope and started exploring her vagina with the help of a lantern, fingered her and sucked her to a climax. From the room inside, the older brother masturbating furiously, shouted: 'Go on, give it to her. If you can't, bring her to me. The bitch!' Suchi wriggled. She screamed. Madan covered her tiny mouth with the filthy cheese cloth, the one he used to wipe both the seat of the rickshaw and his sweat while cycling. Finally she started enjoying the love-making, with a sense of deep shame and utter disgust. Her husband was twenty-two years old and Suchi nine. To be precise, she was exactly nine years and seven months.

Suchi went on detesting the man she was married to. After a little while she also got bored with the nightly rituals, bored being made to do things, at the pleasure when it was no pleasure to her at all. Madan became more and more active. He started pinching and squeezing her flat button nipples. It hurt like hell. At one point, sucking her vagina, Madan got carried away and bit her vulva off. She screamed blue murder, kicked Madan on his deformed genitalia and leapt up. She then jumped over thc verandah and ran to the other end of the slum, all the while screaming her head off.

The neighbourhood believed in the philosophy of live and let live. A few screams, drunken brawls, wife bashing or child battering were quite in order. That night, however, Suchi's flood of loud screams, her crying, and shouting of choicest invectives proved to be too disturbing even for the stoic neighbours.

One woman came out, then the next and the next soon even a few men encircled Suchi. They all tried to fathom what exactly had taken place to bring the brawl out into the open in the middle of the night. In the dim light of the street they could make out Suchi in the nude; jumping up and down with one of her hands clutching her private part. An enterprising smuggler flashed his powerful torchlight on her. He flashed it again and again and kept it on to the crowd's morbid satisfaction.

People could see that the girl's whole body had come out in blotches and that blood was seeping through her legs. One woman gasped and muffled her laughter. Another blurted out, 'Oh, it's nothing. The poor girl has got the curse!' A subdued knowing laughter rippled through the crowd. Menfolk were asked to leave the scene promptly. 'Beat it, this is women's business,' they were told.

Suchi did not laugh. She did not giggle. She shouted at the departing men and the women in a piercing, shrill voice. Opening her legs, she showed the women what her so-called husband had done to her. What's more, she stunned the crowd by telling them that her husband was a *hijra*, and that the *hijras* should come and drag him into their colony. Curse indeed! They should curse her bloody in-law's family and beat them to pulp. Yes, they should. Why the hell were they gaping at her, 'For God's sake, go and get them!' she shrieked.

One woman gently took Suchi to her hovel as she refused to go to the hospital. 'No one comes alive from the hospital', all-knowing Suchi declared. The woman was rather disappointed not to get any more details from the girl. However, she nursed her and gave her shelter for a few days. When Suchi was ready to go, she left. She rubbed off the last traces of vermillon on her head and broke the remaining red conchshell bangles. She unmarried herself and she felt good. She felt clean and free. For the first time since the incident she giggled while she was breaking the bangles and crushing them with a masala grinding stone.

The bus was packed. Someone gave Suchi a helping hand and she managed to squeeze a place for herself by the driver. She told him that she had no money but that she must go to Dimna, to her home. She hummed a tune all the way to her village. She was happy enough to get back to the open sky, where the trees swayed with the wind, the birds sang, and the river flowed ...

The bush telegraph had already reached the family ahead of Suchi's arrival. The brothers gave her a curious look, the mother slapped her own forehead, cursing her fate; the father gave her a weak smile, wondering what would happen next to this wayward, unfortunate daughter of his. The mother could not get much out of Suchi. She massaged her hair with oil. Suchi however, would neither take her frock off or let her massage her body. No amount of persuasion or bullying could make Suchi reveal any details of her married life. All she said was that they were 'badmash' and that Madan was a *hijra*. At times she would get away from her mother's inquistion and go missing for hours. At others she would just giggle. 'You shameless creature' the mother would throw her hands in despair, 'How you can laugh, I can never understand. Your in-laws have thrown you out of their house. Any other girl would have hung her head in shame and stay put.' Wriggling out of the uncomfortable situation Suchi would sing: 'I've run away from the nasties.' 'That's worse', the mother would remind her.

Suchi went about as if nothing had happened – no marriage, no torture, as if no trauma had taken place. But complaints started pouring in once again and so did the thrashing. The mother took her back to the old employer's house. They were, of course, delighted to have her back, warning her that should she go missing as she had earlier, she would be sacked on the spot. 'There!' Suchi giggled.

In no time she sang, she danced, she ran up and down the stairs, she dived into the river with her frock and knickers on. For her, life was once again full of fun. She scrubbed, she brushed and mopped the floor, she jumped up and down with the lever to get water out of the tubewell. She fed the cows and the goats; made cow-dung cakes slapping the cow-dung on the tree trunk. She was the same old Suchi –serving at the tea stall, stealing fruits, sharing the spoils with her father and her little sister when she went home late in the afternoons.

Time went by, her flat chest started to swell up nicely. The teacher's wife gave her a washed rag and told her how to tie herself up with it when she started menstruating. For good measure she gave her some advice. She told her to be wery of men and strangers who may try to befriend her. Suchi looked at her and ran away, giggling till tears ran down her cheeks. 'It is no laughing matter,' she was told. She was much too young and innocent to know the ways of the world.

The womenfolk tried to drum into her ears that she was no longer a little girl. She should act her age, watch how other girls behaved. In fact, Suchi never had much time for girls of her own age and found them all alike – silly and a whine. As for the boys, they usually shooed her away whenever she wanted to play with them. Suchi was content to remain by herself. She loved children though and she would entertain them by singing and dancing. She mimicked the Hindi film stars and dancing girls. She taught them how to gyrate their tiny hips and when the teacher's wife caught her at it, she got a good telling off. Pouting and then bursting out in laughter, she ran away with the children like a pied piper.

After Suchi came back from her hermphrodite husband, the stoker brother-in-law of the brick-field made himself scarce for a while. The stoker had watched Suchi growing up, wearing saris. He scratched his crotch and an idea flashed in his brain. Brilliant. He congratulated himself on his cleverness. God had given him a chance to make big money. 'Thank you, Ma Lakxmi, I will offer you a special puja. If and when I clinch the deal', he promised the deity before he left home.

In the local brick-field, a lot of Biharis from the neighbouring state came to do seasonal work. Some of the men from Bihar happened to fancy Bengali girls – their graceful softness, their gentle curves. What's more, the men were willing to pay a good price to get them.

One afternoon, when the mother-in-law was having her well-deserved siesta, the stoker son-in-law came with a new proposal. He was a persuasive man. He argued that no Bengali man in his senses would marry a once-married girl and certainly they wouldn't touch a divorced girl with a barge pole. However, Suchi was a grown woman now, anything could happen to her. 'People have already started talking. Haven't they? She has nothing upstairs, has she?' He touched his head. 'This man, Ramlal, has seen Suchi at the tea stall. He wants to marry her. Not only marry, he is willing to pay money too. Three thousand rupees! What do you say?' He eyed his mother-in-law from the corner of his eyes. Had she fallen for it or hadn't she? 'Women are greedy, aren't they?' he said to himself.

Suchi's mother could not believe her ears. Three thousand rupees for a girl like Suchi! There had to be a catch somewhere. Why, she got only rupees one thousand and five hundred for her son when she got him married, one cow, and a bicycle which turned out to be a second-hand one. But to get three thousand for her abandoned, retarded daughter was unthinkable. Why, she could buy a piece of land with that sort of money, could she not? Who can tell, her husband might leave his infernal bed and start working once again. Her mind boggled. The stoker forgot to tell his mother-in-law that it was not three but five thousand rupees. He was going to keep two thousand rupees as his commission. Women do not understand business deals, he told himself.

The mother-in-law fought with the greed of becoming a land-owner mentally. She came out with some hard questions. The son-in-law answered her without batting an eyelid. He told her that the prospective bridegroom had land as large as the village, Dimna. He had no sisters to torture Suchi. Only an ailing mother and three younger, loving brothers. But why was he still a bachelor, a man aged twenty seven. 'Poor man, he lost his wife at child-birth.' How far is Bihar? Oh, not far at all. A little further away from Calcutta, he said. Not being a scholar, the stoker had no idea where Bihar was. He had surmised that if the Biharis came to work every year to this brick-field, then Bihar couldn't be that far away. Was he a Hindu? Certainly, he is a pucca Hindu.

When the stoker thought the inquisition was over, and he was about to take his leave, the mother sprung another possible problem to him. She said: 'You know Ramkrishna's daughter, Shanti, don't you? Didn't he also take a bride-price and get his daughter married to this man from Haryana or some such place. Do you remember, how this man settled down in Dimna, but as soon as Shanti gave birth to a girl child, he promptly went back to his first family, back to his country. Now Ramakanta is saddled not only with his deserted daughter but also with the grand-child. This could happen to my Suchi too, no?'

'Ah!' he said. This one was easy. 'Didn't I tell you that our man is going back to Bihar next week?' The stoker softened his voice: 'You'll see Suchi is going to be a rich woman. Richer than your smuggler son-in-law' he laughed. 'Let me think it over.' The mother said at last. 'All right' the stoker said hiding his impatience. 'Don't take too long. Remember, this is our last opportunity as far as Suchi is concerned.' Stupid woman, he murmured under his breath. He said aloud. 'With three thousand rupees you could even buy a piece of land. Think of that. Fate will take care of Suchi.'

Curiously enough, Suchi did not resist her second marriage. She had accepted her mother's assertion that marriage was the only state of being for a woman. What about a widow or a woman deserted by her husband? Suchi had asked. Well, they were married in the first place, were they not? her mother had replied But then, I was married too, wasn't I? Suchi had said. He was not a man, as it turned out, was he? the mother had pointed out.

At the brief wedding ceremony Suchi did not look bashful. Defying conventional modesty, she looked at her husband with frank curiosity. The sisters hissed: 'Lower your gaze.' To Suchi he looked a middle-aged man like the teacher she worked for. Would he be kind like her father, she wondered. Whenever mother beat her up, father would shout from his bed telling her that it was not the right way to discipline a child. Why does this man look so grim? she asked herself. Suchi's mother looked at her son-in-law's rich moustache and shuddered for no reason. She groped for Suchi's hands and pressed them, trying to comfort her or perhaps herself. Suchi smiled back at her. 'Poor girl, she does not understand what life is all about', the mother thought.

THREE CHAPTER

At the age of fifteen, bigamous Suchi set off for her second husband's home. It was a remote village in Bihar where electricity had yet to reach.

The lessons started on the train. Ramlal painstakingly lectured her as to how she should behave in his village. For a start, he asked her to cover her head with her sari. 'What? What did you say?' she asked him in Bengali, pretending not to understand Hindi. She hated covering her head. She had felt hot and bothered when she had had to, during the wedding ceremony. He repeated his injunction in broken Bengali. Suchi looked at him uncomprehendingly, then turned her face and smothered her giggle. Ramlal shook her by the shoulder; all the people in the compartment looked at the man disapprovingly. He dropped his hands. However, he was not easily put off. He told her what was expected of her. Suchi understood alright. Obedience was the key word. She must forget her shameless Bengali ways, must obey and serve her husband, her three brothers-in-law and above all her mother-in-law. Period. 'No lazying or frolicing about, understand?'

This was the first time in her life Suchi was riding a train. She was thrilled. No way was she going to get intimidated by this man's sombre, threatening voice. How wonderful it was to ride a train. She wished her little sister was with her. The train would move very fast at times and slowly, really slowly, at others. She was going somewhere, anywhere, she did not care as long as she was on the train. It zig-zagged through the changing landscape, from the lush green fields to harsh, hilly, dusty places. She loved the rocking, the sound of the train, its speed, it's slow pace as it neared the stations; the bursting of a cacophony of sounds as masses of people scrambled to get into it; squatters on the platforms – eating, drinking, sleeping, gossiping, laughing, quarreling; the insistent cry of the beggars and hawkers –chaa-chaa-chayee. 'Could she have a cup of tea, please?' Ramlal obliged. He could not be such a bad man after all, Suchi thought. She gave him a dazzling smile, her small, even teeth gleamed in the retiring sun. Ramlal, with his big bulk, looked down at her impassively. Disappointed, Suchi transferred her happy smile to the passengers. They smiled back. Ramlal angirily nudged her with his elbow. Suchi promptly moved down with a family of six children, who had made themselves at home on the floor. The whole compartment shook with shrieks of laughter. Suchi had a whale of a time sharing their food and water. Life is full of fun, she thought.

There is a saying in Bengali that after laughter comes tears. But Suchi did not cry in the bullock-cart, though she felt forlorn and much too exhausted to enjoy the sights of the villages they went past. She slept, slept right through and reached the home of her in-laws in the early hours of the morning.

Thankfully, she was left to her own devices for a couple of days. She helped her mother-in-law to cook, learnt to make chapatis, washed the floor and fed the buffaloes, and softly sang Bengali hit-songs. She giggled when her brothers-in-law spoke to her in Hindi.

On the fourth day, when the brothers came home, the mother-in-law told her to wash and wipe their feet with the cheese cloth; following that, to massage their bodies. And by turn, they came home during the day, walking miles from the field, ostensibly to be massaged by Suchi. When the massage turned into attempted rape she fought like a tigress. She screamed and shouted filthy words in Bengali and nearly scratched their eyes off. Her mother-in-law pretended not to hear.

At nights Ramlal would beat her up for disobeying his younger brothers' instructions to massage them and then violate her unmercifully. When she fought back defiantly he would tie her long dark wavy hair to the wooden pillar of the room for the night. When she wasn't nodding off, she would scream the whole night long. Now, the day-time fracas became too much for the ailing mother-in-law. She just couldn't understand why a chit of a Bengali girl refused to 'massage' her sons. Ramlal had, after all, paid five thousand rupees for this skinny, silly girl, hadn't he? In her younger days she herself had had to go through the same ritual. In her case, it was her father-in-law. Look at Draupadi, did she not serve her five husbands without a murmur? Didn't the Mahabharata extoll the virtues of Draupadi? Fed up with the daily screaming and fuss, she grabbed Suchi by her plait and took her to the field. Now get on with it, if that's what you like.

It was hard, it was very hard to begin with, but my word was she relieved to be freed from the clutches of her three brothers-in-law! She cut the wheat with a sickle, carried them in a bunch in her hands to the mud-house, spread the wheat in the courtyard, scrambled them in the sun, sifted them and pressed them in the home-made machine, making them ready for dough. When she came home, she washed her hands and feet, then rolled seventy chapatis, fluffed them up on the open fire and served them hot. Her hands, her shoulders, thighs and back, her legs and indeed each part of her body ached and gradually turned hard, strong and rounded. Her breasts became full, thrusting out like two rocks. The brothers-in-law's hands and loins became itchy but before the onslaught could start Ramlal took her off to Amritsar. He had had enough of the brick-fields in Bengal. Besides, Suchi might refuse to come back to Bihar with him from Dimna.

Suchi was grateful beyond words. She thought to herself, Ramlal was a good man to take her away from that evil house. She promised to herself that she would become good, obedient, docile like the teacher's wife in Dimna. 'I'll be good', she told herself.

Chapter Four

In Amritsar, Ramlal started selling vegetables on a mobile cart. At the end of the day, he would usually come home drunk. Once in a while, when he was less inebriated, he would play with Suchi's body like a cat with a mouse. He would grab her breasts with his two strong hands, kneading them all the while making a running commentary about how she should knead dough to make chapatis. He would poke her here and there. He would stub his bidi on her back and then kiss the spot with his saliva. When Suchi cried out in pain, he would tickle her armpits, or the sole of her feet.

Suchi would giggle helplessly and scream: 'Stop it. Please stop it.' He would cover her mouth with his dirty hand till Suchi's eyes would bulge out and she would start choking in her saliva.

While eating his supper at night, he would pick up a fight. Dangling a chapati between two of his fingers, he would say, 'Do you call this thing, a chapati? This is your Bangla chapati, shove it down your bloody throat. You bitch!' Then he would throw the chapati at her and turn the plate full of cooked meal upside down. He would stagger up to the bed, stripping himself, barking out orders for Suchi to join him at once. Without a preamble he would lift her sari and force himself into her. And even before the semen stopped dripping he would start snoring on her sprawling body. Suchi would curse her mother for not having smothered her at birth. `Why didn't you?' She would cry out in the dark, trying to dislodge the leaky mountain on top of her body.

Yes, indeed, the fights seemed to have beaten every ounce of verve out of Suchi. Now, she only sobbed night and day. She could not talk to anyone, their language was so strange, the well-built men and women appeared to her to be so aggressive and hard.

Suchi and Ramlal were tenants of an older couple. The Sikh landlady had heard the muffled screams and the helpless giggles. After seeing Suchi in the mornings, she concluded that the giggles she heard every night were not of joy. She mentioned that to her husband, only to be told to mind her own business. Undeterred, the landlady started befriending the girl. She said, 'My son is a big businessman, he owns a shop larger than this house. He lives in Southall, you know. It's the most beautiful place in London. We'll visit them next summer.' She showed her pictures of her son, daughter-in-law and her grand-children. To Suchi, Southall sounded like the Santals at Dimna! She understood her broken Hindi. She started calling her chachiji and her husband chachaji. Soon she became part of the couple's everyday life. She had her meals with them on the days Ramlal told her he was not coming home for lunch.

They took her to the golden temple. That was the first time she was really seeing Amritsar. Her joy and curiosity knew no bounds. She felt like dancing about the place, splashing water from the huge tank. She was awed by the huge complex, by the golden dome, by the great book, the Granth Sahib, that was placed on a throne, and to which the Sikhs prayed. It was nothing like the Gods and Goddesses they had back home. No matter. She prayed fervently to the Great Book. She begged, 'God of the Sikhs, please send me back to my village, Dimna. Just once ... please.' One by one tears dropped on the marble floor of the temple. She stood up slowly and smiled at chachiji. Chachiji pressed her hand and whispered 'God will answer your prayer, my child.'

The next morning before he went off to work, chachiji had got hold of Ramlal. She told him that Suchi was looking quite ill lately; could he not send her to her parents just for few weeks? Ramlal grumbled. He said that there was nothing wrong with his wife. She was plain lazy like all Bengalees. Chachiji pointed out gently,'Don't you see the dark circles under her eyes?' Ramlal said that it had nothing to do with being unwell; she slept all day and night, what else had she to do in the house? 'But she has lost a lot of weight since she came here', Chachiji persisted. Ramlal told them he did not earn fancy money to send his wife for a holiday like rich people. Chachaji remarked mildly, 'I will pay her fare. She has become like our daughter, you see'. 'I'll think it over,' Ramlal left for work, muttering under his breath.

That night, Ramlal raped her viciously.

The next morning, she could hardly get off the khatia to make breakfast for him. Before he went off to work, he told Chachiji that he had decided to send Suchi back home with one of his friends. The lady said: 'God bless you.' She went to give the news to the girl. Suchi's whole body ached but she cried out with joy. She fell at Chachiji's feet and she wouldn't let go of them. Chachiji bent down and took Suchi in her arms, kissed her forehead, and murmured: 'God bless you my child'. Suchi held her tightly and sobbed on her shoulders. Never in her life had she experienced such tenderness and she never would again. Before she left the house, Chachiji gave her a packet of chapatis, dry vegetable-curry and pickles for the train journey and added some dry fruits.

Once again she would ride a train. The *rel-gari* with so many bogies would take her back to her village, Dimna. She smiled to herself. There was no seat to be had. Like a veteran traveller she plonked the suitcase on the floor of the compartment and sat on it. She longed for the train to move. The carriage was more than full, why then this wait at the platform? Buses never wait, do they?

Her companion, Ramlal's friend Laloo found a seat alright. They started chatting ninteen to the dozen and she took an instant dislike to the man who was going to escort her to Dimna. He was weezy, with shifty eyes and a peculiar lop-sided smile. Whenever he laughed, the saliva of the chewing grass trickled down his chin. Disgusting. She looked around the carriage, spotted a baby clinging to her mother's breast and quite a few children sitting quietly in other places. She knew instantly that she was going to have a great time. For a moment she felt a pang of guilt. She should not be so pleased to leave her husband behind, should she? 'After all, it was kind of him to send me to Dimna', she said to herself. The whistle blew. Ramlal stood up in front of Suchi and said: 'Listen to Laloo, do as he tells you, understand?' he said and jumped off the running train.

Suchi's first thought was that she was free to enjoy the train journey on her own. She ignored her escort completely. In no time, she made friends with the children, shared her food with them and they with her. For two nights, two of the children slept with her on the floor of the compartment. On the third day Laloo, the escort, told Suchi to get ready. 'We will be getting off soon,' he said. It seemed every one was getting ready to get off with them. 'Which station is it?' Suchi asked one of the co-passengers. 'Patna', he said. 'Patna? Why Patna?' Ah! they would have to change the train for Calcutta, wouldn't they? And from Calcutta, to Dimna. She thanked the Sikh Book once again.

'When is the next train to Calcutta?' Suchi asked Laloo . It was the first time she had spoken to him without looking at his dribbling mouth. 'Come, hurry, the bus will be leaving any minute,' Laloo said, rushing off towards the gate. Confused, Suchi ran after him.

At the bus stop, Laloo snatched Suchi's suitcase and clambered on to the bus. Once he had made some space for themselves he came down to hurry Suchi. 'What are you waiting for?'

Suddenly suspicious, she said: 'This bus is not going to Calcutta, is it?' 'Of course, it isn't.' Laloo stretched his hand to pull her up.

She screamed in Hindi: 'Don't you dare

touch me. I am not going with you' she added some abuse in Bengali.

The bus driver had started the powerful engine, throbbing with impatience to begin the journey. The bus moved an inch or two, as if to say 'We mean business. Get on in, you fools.'

The passengers were getting impatient too. After a long arduous journey, all they wanted was to get home. Not that they did not enjoy a little drama, but this was not the time for it. Laloo jumped off the bus, went around where Suchi was standing and tried to push her up the steps. In her agitation Suchi shrieked in Bengali: 'This man is abducting me. Stop him please.' No one understood a word. The driver started honking, the conductor asked Laloo what she was going on about. Laloo touched his head to indicate that the woman was off her rocker. The conductor in a swift movement got hold of Suchi's hand, pulled her up and shoved her in. The passengers cheered. Laloo jumped on to the running bus. Off it went. Suchi was pushed through the barricade of men, women, children and goats and with a final shove she was made to sit on top of her tin suitcase placed on a seat.

Suchi sat dazed. Her mind went totally blank. Laloo sat close to her. The bus waded through the crowded road, honking, the conductor shouting at the pedestrian: 'Hat jao, hat jao.' It gathered speed once it left the crowd, rattling and sputtering on a road full of pot-holes.

Laloo put his arm around Suchi as if to protect her from toppling over. Suchi sat still. The young conductor came for the fare and asked him if his wife was alright now. 'She looks ill,' he said. As soon as the conductor left for another passenger, Laloo put his hand on Suchi's thrusting breast under the sari so that no one could see what he was up to. The next moment, Laloo found himself thrown below, entangled in people's feet. The children started laughing, the young women giggled. Suchi had come alive. She spat at him. The passengers felt sorry for Laloo – one never knew what a mad women would do. They helped Laloo to stand on his feet. He gave them an embarrassed smile and glared at Suchi.

The last lap of the journey was by a bullock-cart. Suchi did not allow Laloo to sit with her under the canopy.

'Wait till I write to Ramlal,' Laloo said.

Suchi ignored him. Wretched Suchitra kept telling herself that she should have known better. Suddenly she saw everything clearly. Ramlal had never married her. He went through the charade only to fob her family off. He had bought her body, he had bought a slave. The slave should serve him in any way he wanted. She should serve his mother and his brothers. He merely chuckled whenever she told him about his brother's sexual harassment, or when she tried to fill up the details. She felt certain now that Ramlal knew everything and did not care. She shook her head. No way, she told herself, no way would she allow the monsters to rape and ravage her body. She could always kill herself – jump in the well in the courtyard of the house, could she not? The thought almost cheered her up. No, no, she should kill them first. She could at least kill one of them. She did not see any problem with that. What about the other two, and the mother-in-law? The brothers were always together laughing, joking, slapping each other, wrestling in mock fights. Even so, if she killed one of them, that would scare the others. No? No, I would have to kill myself. The thought no longer made her feel good. She sat in utter despair, staring but seeing nothing of the slumberous, dusty village road, or feeling the discomfort of the hard seat of the cart, the jolting and the tossing. She did not even hear the cart-driver's muttering,'hut, hut', or the sound of his cane smashing into the bullocks body.

An idea struck her. She almost smiled. It should work, she told herself. With the hope of a drowning person, she finally dozed off.

The three brothers-in-law were, of course, delighted to see her back on her own. They smacked their lips, slapped their dhoti clad thighs, playfully fingered their crotch and laughed a drunken laugh. No need to come home during the day any more. The night was young and long. Without a word spoken, they knew that they were going to take turns, starting with the eldest.

Mother-in-law was glad, too, to have the helping hand back. She felt she was getting too old to run errands and feed her hungry brood. She let Suchi sleep in the bed next to her that night. Suchi was grateful to the old woman for that. The day after, it was another story. The old woman insisted that she sleep in her own room.

Why did she want to send her to the hungry wolves? She was a woman. Could she not feel what it is like to be raped? Then? Did she want her to be the plaything of her sons? Was that it? 'We shall see.' Suchi looked grim and stopped talking to the old woman. Before she went to bed she massaged her body generously with a large amount of mustard oil. The mud hut did not have any doors excepting the rear and front ones with bolts. She waited, her heart thumping, holding her angry tears back.

The fighting spirit had come back to Suchi.

The eldest one entered the room, having just enough alcohol in his belly and fire between his legs to overcome her. Suchi, however, glided through his powerful hands and legs like a slippery cobra. The almost silent, fierce struggle soon left the man exhausted. She pushed him with all her might, he fell off the wooden ropy khatia and lay on the floor, snoring, all night. Suchi covered her naked body with her sari and slept, alert.

The two brothers next door heard the grunts, the loud hissing sounds. It got them excited thinking that at last their sister-in-law had succumed to the charm of their brother. They masturbated furiously on the khatia. Next morning, they gave meaningful looks and satisfied smiles at their brother. He nodded, smiling back.

These – almost silent but fierce fights – lasted for another two nights, with a few variations here and there. It only established his virility in the eyes of the other brothers.

It was, alas, too good to last. The three brothers in a drunken garrulity confessed their inability to prove their manhood to a fifteen-years-old girl. Shame on them. They sat huddled, conspired, combing their mustache with their index fingers. Satisfied, they smiled and slapped each other.

In the middle of the night, they took Suchitra completely by surprise. Covering her mouth they bundled her off and out of the house to a nearby bush. Her frantic thrashings and throttled screams were of no use. They finally pinned her down. One held her head, the other both her sprawling legs, the third entered her, squeezing and kneading her breasts like dough, breaking the skin of her black rose nipples. They got carried away, however, by their triumph. They felt great, they felt powerful – like Ravana. They laughed their drunken laugh. They slapped each other like the wrestlers do. When the time came for the second round for the three brothers, Suchi managed to free herself. She jumped and ran, ran for her life in the dark moonless night. The brothers chased but lost her.

She took cover in a sugar-cane bush, panting, bleeding from head to toe; tears blinding her eyes but she did not stop running. She could run no longer. She stumbled. She fell unconscious.

At the crack of dawn, one woman from the village came to defecate with a *lota* full of water and found her naked body –battered, bitten and bloodied. At first sight, she thought it was a dead body. There were clear marks on her throat. She was about to summon help, when, luckily for Suchi, the woman's sense of modesty won the day. She covered her body with a dupatta and as she touched her, she found that the body was still warm. She felt her nose with her cheek, and generously sprinkled her face with water. She revived Suchi.

Eventually, Suchi limped back with the help of the woman to her home nearby. She sat down, huddled in the courtyard, unable to move.

The woman washed her, nursed her, did everything without questioning her. Suchi, her head bent, told the woman in fits and starts, about her three brothers-in-law. The woman heard her quietly, rocking on her seat, looking at the distant blue hills, listening immersed in her own thoughts.

After a few days, the woman took Suchi back to her mother-in-law. She told her that Suchi was badly hurt, she must be left alone. She would come round everyday to check if she was alright or else ...

The brothers-in-law left Suchi's swollen, bruised body alone. The village woman came everyday and fed her. One day, she brought two post-cards. Suchi wrote to her brother in Bengali. The woman wrote in Hindi to Ramlal in Amritsar. The message was simple, 'I am very ill. Please come at once.'

CHAPTER FIVE

She waited. She gained strength day by day and she waited. Word came that Ramlal was on his way.

She smiled. Her broken lips still hurt. She

bathed carefully by the well. She wore a fresh sari and started cooking for her husband. She sang a Bengali hit song, an imitation of a Hindi one "*Ami tomake bhalobashi,* I love you, I love you." She forgot his cruelty to her. She forgot Ramlal's deceptions – sending her back to the evil house. Her only thought was that he was coming to rescue her. Her hero. He might even be going back to work in the Dimna brick-field. Wouldn't that be wonderful? 'I would love him, I would' Suchi promised and hoped. And she indulged in her favourite past time – day-dreaming.

In a leisurely way the images moved before her eyes; to Suchi they seemed more real than the open fire, right in front of her, glowing on her weather-beaten face. *The sky was ever so blue with bright clouds floating. With her hair flying in the air she was running through the golden-green wheat-field in slow motion to meet her husband transformed into Mithun Chakraborty or is it Rajesh Khanna? One or the other was coming towards her with his arms outstretched to enfold her in his heavenly bosom. He was touching her. Laughingly, picking her up and lowering her gently, bending down to kiss her on her ripe lips, full of sweet sugarcane juice.* Eyes misty, she hummed softly: 'I love you'. She bent her head to knead the dough and she sang: '*Ami tomake bhalobashi –*'

Suddenly she felt a violent tug on her bunch of luxurious hair. She was being pulled straight up with a jerk. Her legs tried to balance and they kicked the earthen pot full of rice, into pieces. It burnt her bare feet.

Who? What? Her broken romance squeaked.

Her husband was beating her with great fury with his bare fists, bruising his own knuckles. 'So, harami, daughter of a Bengali bitch. You wouldn't obey my brothers, my only mother. I'll kill you today. I'll stop you from telling tales to our neighbors forever.'

At first Suchi was too shocked to fight back. A couple of times, she tried to tell him that he must listen to her first. She gave up. Instead, all her energy went to cover her body with her hands as she ran up and down in an attempt to protect herself.

She did not scream. She gasped for breath. Her ribs broke, her kidney was hurt, her jaw squeezed into a pulp, her nose bled, her eyes swelled up, and two front teeth went missing. In a final act of defiance, she spat blood at her husband and collapsed on top of the dough, the vegetable curry, the rice-pudding and the broken earthen pot.

Enough was enough! Mother-in-law stepped in, took one look at Suchi and then at her son's blood-stained kurta and screamed in a hoarse whisper: 'She is dying. Take her to the doctor. Let her die there. We will be in police trouble again. Quick.'

Now, the police was bad news – next to the local mafias – in Bihar. It could result in selling off the land to bribe them and their higher-ups, but even then it may be difficult to save one's neck. They had gone through the nightmare once before, they knew the works. Breathing hard, Ramlal stood still for a moment, looked at his mother with blood-shot eyes, stared at Suchi's bleeding, swollen face, and the torn bunch of dark hair floating in the rice-pudding. He loved Bengali rice-pudding. He kicked her and she rolled over. 'Ramlal' an urgent whisper from the mother, 'Pick her up. Get rid of her at the doctor's door, at once. Do what I say! Tell them that she has fallen from the roof, tell them anything. Go'. Silently and without a word, Ramlal picked Suchi's unconscious body up and ran towards the local health centre.

Luckily for Suchi, the doctor was a young man who had recently joined the Health service. He took one look at Suchi and called the police. He did what he could for Suchitra, and detained her at the makeshift hospital. The police, in front of the doctor, got a confession from Ramlal, in case Suchi died. They also got him to sign and agree that he would take her back to her mother, should she live. The local police were pleased as punch to pin Ramlal down once again.

Suchitra survived. Her brother came and took her back to Dimna from the Health Centre. Four weeks later Ramlal followed her to claim his 'lawful' wife back. Now Suchitra went straight to the Dimna Panchayat Secretary and told him briefly what he needed to know. The village council called a meeting. They sat in a circle under a banyan tree. For the first time in the Panchayat's history both the Communist Party (Marxist) and the Congress (I) concurred. Suchi must not be sent back to her in-law's only to be beaten to death by some 'khotta goondas'. Should Ramlal agree to settle down in this Bengali village under the watchful eyes of the Council, only then would Suchi go back to her husband.

Suchi vigorously shook her head. She told the council that in no circumstances was she going to live with a Bihari goonda. Bengali chauvinism won the day. Suchi's life was saved.

She went home with her mother, humming a tune, with a spring in her steps. At night when she was about to hit the sack, the older brother came and told her that Ramlal wanted to have a word with her. He wasn't too pleased that his sister would stay behind with them. Suchi came out promptly and asked: 'What do you want?' 'I want to take you home' Ramlal said. He promised that he would never touch her in anger. She would not have to massage his brothers any more. Suchi told him calmly: 'Go and fuck your brothers.' Ramlal threatened to drag her by her hair or what was left of it. Then he made a mistake, he turned to the brother, shouting: 'I am not going to go back empty-handed, give me back my five thousand rupees!' That did it. Giving money back was altogether a different proposition and five thousand rupees. Impossible! The cheek of the man, he thought. The house-holders were unaware that the stoker had pocketed two thousand rupees as his brokerage fee. The brother shouted back and told him that if he did not leave the premises at once, he would get the villagers to beat him to death. 'Fuck off', he said, 'S-aalaa!'

By this time, the neighbours had come out with sticks and kitchen knives. Ramlal left, fuming, threatening dire consequences should he not get his money back. Suchi spat at his retreating back. The marriage was truly over as far as she was concerned.

Chapter Six

Suchitra went back to her former employer's house. The village shook its head and wondered what really was wrong with the girl. Her mother couldn't keep her, two wedded husbands couldn't tame this wild girl. That the second one couldn't be the husband according to the law of the land or for that matter, that she was 'married' twice under-age never bothered the village. It was, they concluded, her destiny to remain barren and single. The village chose to forget Suchi.

Suchitra has bounced back to her old cheerful self. She still giggles. She runs up and down the stairs. She dives the pond instead of into the river, fully clothed. She does not climb trees. She pumps the tube-well, bending, with her strong hand. She does not go to the tea-stall any more either. More teasing, another joke is added to the employer's family stock. Suchi ran away because she had to massage her Bihari brothers-in-law. Ha! Ha! Suchi laughs with them with the sari covering her mouth.

No one knows, or cares that Suchi gets so mad from time to time. They, the house-holders and her own family, choose to see her laughing face, hear her humming a tune. They conclude that she is contented with life. She never talks about her past or about her future, as if, she is suspended in time. Her world, away from the prying eyes, is a world of celluloid day-dreams.

She has one passion. She loves watching Hindi films. She finds Bengali films much too soppy. She likes the action-packed films, where there is danger, risk, violence, dancing round the trees, prancing on the open fields and above all, the romance and the glamour. The teacher, the head of the family strongly objects to Hindi films. So Suchi sneaks out to the village video parlour, sits on the mat and watches the beautiful people. The bewitching heroines are no push-overs. They fight back on their own or with the help of their lovers. She gets immense pleasure in seeing the *badmash*, the evil man getting beaten up and smashed to pulp. She angrily whispers: 'Kill them, kill them.' Her hands twitch, involuntarily, to throttle the last breath out of the *shaitans*. When the loving couple end up in sweet embrace, she cries her eyes out. Those are happy tears. She walks back to her employer's house, looking remote with thoughts brimming with dreams. Her eyes do not invite any young men.

In the eyes of the village she has become untouchable. There has to be something terribly wrong in her character to invite violence and rape. The older villagers recall Suchi's first husband. Was he really a *hijra* or had she made the story up to run away from him? As for the second husband, they could well believe, a Bihari khotta doing all kinds of things, but they do wonder. As for Suchi, she appears to be quite unconcerned as to what people thought about her.

With her sturdy, buxom body she comes back to the teacher's house. She silently gets on with her chores. When she is in that kind of a mood, the family leaves her alone. If anyone, by mistake raises his or her voice, she snaps back like a hissing snake. Otherwise she is the same old Suchi, cooking the meals on record time, running up and down the stairs, eyes dancing with mischief. She laughs at her own jokes, and from time to time she bursts out into the latest Hindi hit songs.

There are a few differences between now and then. Instead of going home in the afternoons she sleeps at the teacher's house. She has got an attic room which is also a store room. She is able to claim only one of its wall, which she has covered with picture cut-outs of her favourite heroes and heroines of the Hindi films. There is one other crucial difference, she is allowed to keep her own wages, which has gone up from fifteen to fifty rupees per month.

She loves the roof top, even in the heat of summer. It is her own space, however stuffy and crowded with junk it may be. For the first time in her life, she has a space to herself, away from prying eyes. Occasionally, sleep eludes her. Why has fate been so cruel to her, she wonders.

Restless, she unlocks the door to the roof and breathes deeply in the open. All the gloom and sense of doom disappear in the beautiful night, her heart slowly fills with the sheer joy of living. She absorbs the dark silence of the night. Against the pitch black sky the green trees whisper to each other. She listens to the night talking to her, comforting her. Sometimes the street dogs bark, foxes howl, perhaps a bird shakes its wings or cries out. She looks up. The stars seem to sparkle like frozen tears. She laughs, she dances quietly like her film stars – her full, strong breasts shaking with the rhythm of her light feet. The stars seem to dance with her.

CHAPTER SEVEN

On the roof top, in the night, free of all constraints, her fantasies run riot. She feels as if she is wearing a flowing milk-white dress, studded with stars walking with outstretched hands to meet her beloved. She feels ecstatic. At times though, her hands flop by her sides like a rag doll. Her fingers curl up in fists – the tight fists filled with emptiness – like her dreamless heart.

One night, she quietly goes down the stairs. She does not switch on the light. Like a cat, she can see through the dark. She unbolts the rotting wooden door and walks towards the ghat. She strips herself naked, leaves the key under the folded sari. For a moment she stands still. In the dark night no one can see her scarred, much battered body. Not even the stars in the sky blink. Silently she slips into the water. She embraces the river Didar. Didar that flows steadily with sorrow and joy.

She starts swimming with strong strokes. She loves the cool water, caressing her. She dives deep and then comes up, letting the water roll over her and into her. She feels clean and fresh. With her increasingly tired limbs and body, she starts floating. The river rocks her on its cradle. Her weary eyelids droop. A faint smile plays on her wet lips.

The next morning, some fishermen on a boat see a naked, bloated body of a young woman stuck in one of their fishing poles. Seeing a woman's body in the river is not that shocking, not for fishermen, any way. However, a young woman, naked? They shake their heads in disbelief. No woman in her right mind will kill herself and display her naked body to all and sundry. It must be a case of foul play!

That day is truly ruined. For a worthless wild woman who must have asked for it! One of the older men, voices the dreaded word: 'Police'. He ticks off the young fisherman, 'Stop gloating over it. Go and call the police. Damn! Why get stuck, of all places, in our fishing pole?'